TREASURED TALES

This book belongs to...

....

....

Sleeping Beauty
and
Beauty and The Beast

p

This is a Parragon Book
This edition published in 2001

Parragon
Queen Street House
4 Queen Street
Bath, BA1 1HE, UK

Created by
THE COMPLETE WORKS
St Mary's Road, Royal Leamington Spa, Warwickshire CV31 1JP, UK

ISBN 0-75255-209-0

Sleeping Beauty

Once upon a time, in a land far, far away, there lived a king and queen who were kind and good. When the queen gave birth to a baby girl, the whole kingdom rejoiced.

When it was time for the baby to be christened, the king and queen arranged a great celebration. They asked the seven good fairies of the kingdom to be the baby's godmothers. But eight fairies arrived at the feast.

The eighth fairy was ugly and old, and no one had seen her for years. The king and queen, thinking she was dead, hadn't invited her to take part in the ceremony.

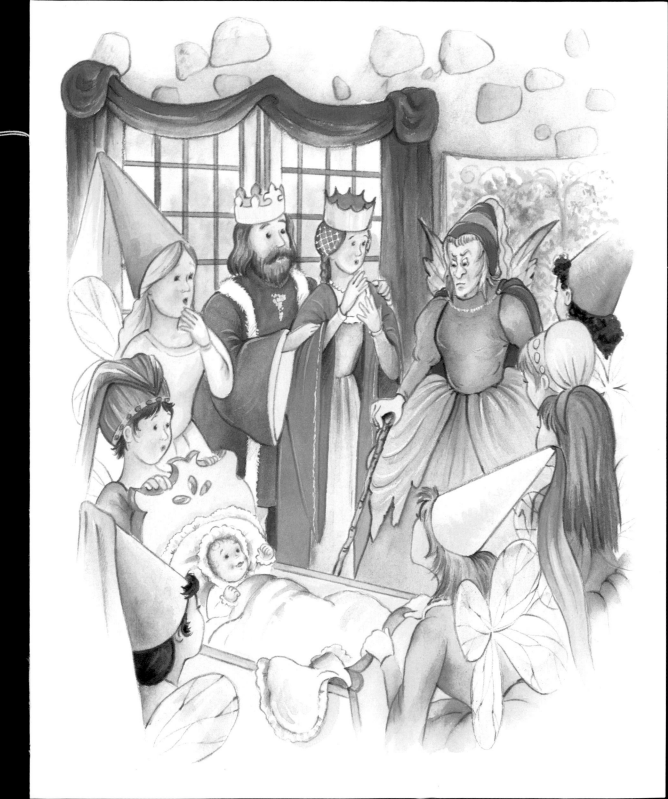

Soon it was time for the fairies to give the baby princess their magical presents. The first gave her the gift of beauty, the second gave her wisdom. The third fairy said she would be graceful, the fourth said that she would dance like the wind. The fifth and sixth gave her the gift of music and song, so that she would sing and play like an angel.

Just before the seventh fairy stepped up to give the princess her gift, the eighth fairy pushed ahead of her. "The princess," she cackled, "will prick her finger on the spindle of a spinning wheel - and die!"

Everyone in the room was horrified, and the queen began to cry. But then the seventh fairy stepped forward. "Here is my gift," she said. "The princess will not die. Instead, when she pricks her finger, she will fall asleep for a hundred years. At the end of that time, a prince will come to wake her up."

The king and queen were relieved, but even so, they ordered every spinning wheel in the kingdom to be destroyed. They couldn't bear to think of anything hurting their daughter.

The years passed and the princess grew into a lovely young girl, as wise, beautiful and graceful as the fairies had promised.

On the day of her sixteenth birthday, she was wandering through the castle when she came to a small room in a tall tower. Inside, an old woman sat spinning thread.

"My dear," cackled the old woman, "come here and try this for yourself."

As soon as the princess's hand touched the spindle, she pricked her finger and fell to the floor in a deep sleep.

When they discovered their daughter, the king and queen were heartbroken, for they knew that she would not wake for a hundred years. They called for the palace guard, who gently laid the sleeping princess on a golden stretcher and carried her to the royal bedchamber. There they placed her on a bed with silken pillows and velvet covers. The king and queen watched over her and cried.

"Oh, my dear," said the queen to her husband. "How are we ever going to cope without our darling daughter?"

The fairy who had saved the princess's life heard what had happened. Worried that the princess would wake up in a world where she knew no one, she cast a spell over the whole castle. Everyone, from the guards and the kitchen maids to the gardeners and the cooks - even the princess's pet dog - fell into a deep, deep sleep.

Then the fairy made tall trees and twisting, sharp brambles grow around the castle, surrounding it with a thick thorny wall that no one could get through. Only the very tops of the castle's towers could be seen.

And so a hundred years went by.

One day, a prince from a nearby land was out riding when he saw the tops of the castle towers rising from the middle of the thick, dark wood. He asked some of the country people about it, and they told him the story of the Sleeping Beauty.

"Many people have wanted to get through those thorns," they told him, "but they have all died trying."

The prince was determined to be the one who succeeded and set off towards the mysterious castle.

To the prince's amazement, the thorny brambles and the twisting branches of the dark trees let him pass through easily. He reached the castle door, and went inside.

The prince walked through many halls and chambers where people and animals slept as if they were dead. He searched every room and chamber, until he found the very one where the beautiful princess slept.

"Oh, princess!" cried the prince. "You are more beautiful than the most delicate rose ever found."

The prince moved quietly towards the sleeping princess and gazed down lovingly at her. He gently took her tiny hand in his, and as love filled his heart, he knelt beside her and slowly kissed her red lips. Instantly the princess's eyes opened.

"Is it you, my prince?" she said, when she saw him. "I have waited such a long time for you!"

At that moment the spell was broken, and everyone else in the castle woke up, too.

That evening, the princess's sixteenth birthday was celebrated with a joyous party - just a hundred years too late!

The princess and her prince danced together all evening, and soon after, were married. They lived together in happiness for many, many years.

Beauty
and the Beast

Once upon a time there was a man who lived in a cottage in the country with his three daughters. His youngest daughter was so pretty that everyone called her "Beauty", which made her two sisters very angry and jealous.

One day the man had to go to the city. Before he left, he told his daughters that he would bring each of them back a present and asked what they would like.

"Jewels!" the eldest daughter demanded. "Silk dresses!" said the second daughter. But all Beauty asked for was a single white rose.

On his return home, the father was caught in a snowstorm and lost his way. The blizzard was so thick and fierce and the forest so large and dark that he nearly gave up hope of ever finding his home. Then, through the mist, he glimpsed a grand palace.

He staggered to the great door - there seemed to be no one about. Inside, he found a table laid with a magnificent dinner. The man ate hungrily, then searched the house. Upstairs, he found a huge bed where he gratefully fell into an exhausted sleep. In the morning, when he awoke, breakfast was waiting beside the bed.

As he set off on his way home he noticed a wonderful rose garden. Remembering Beauty's request, he stopped to pick a white rose. Suddenly, with a mighty roar, a terrifying, snarling Beast appeared.

"I have welcomed you with every comfort," he growled, "and in return you steal my roses!"

Shaking with fear, the man begged for forgiveness. "I only wanted the rose as a present for my daughter!"

"I will spare you," said the Beast, "but only if your daughter comes to live here of her own free will. If not, you must return in three months."

Back home, the man tearfully told his daughters what had happened. To his surprise, Beauty agreed to go.

When she arrived at the palace, a glorious meal was waiting for her. "The Beast must want to fatten me," she thought. But she sat and ate.

As soon as Beauty finished her meal, the Beast appeared. He was truly horrifying, and she was frightened.

"Your room is all ready," said the Beast, and he led her to a door that said "Beauty's Room" in gold letters.

The room was everything Beauty could have wished for. She saw a little piano, beautiful silk dresses and fresh, fragrant roses. On the dressing table was a mirror with these words on it:

If anything you long to see,
Speak your wish, and look in me.

"I wish I could see my father," said Beauty, and instantly saw her father in the mirror, sitting sadly beside the fire at home.

"Perhaps the Beast doesn't mean to kill me after all," Beauty thought. "I wonder what he does want?"

The next evening the Beast joined Beauty for supper. "Tell me," he said, "am I truly horrible to look at?"

Beauty could not lie. "You are," she said. "But I know you are very kind-hearted."

"Then," said the Beast, "will you marry me?"

Beauty was surprised. She knew he might be angry if she refused, but she couldn't say yes as she didn't love him. "No," she said, "I will not marry you."

The Beast sighed so heavily that the walls shook. "Good night, then," he said sadly. And he left her to finish her dinner alone.

Months passed, and the Beast gave Beauty everything she could want. She was very happy in the palace.

Every evening, the Beast asked the same question: "Will you marry me?" And Beauty always said no. But she was growing very fond of him.

One day, Beauty looked in the magic mirror and saw that her father was ill. She begged the Beast to let her go home, and sadly he agreed.

"Take this magic ring," he told her. "If you ever want to come back, put it by your bedside and when you wake up, you will be here."

"I will come back," Beauty promised.

So Beauty went home to look after her father. He was soon well again, and she was ready to go back to the Beast. But her jealous sisters hated to think of Beauty going back to a palace while they lived in a small cottage. So they convinced her to stay a while longer.

One night, Beauty dreamt that the Beast was lying dead in his garden, and she woke up in tears. She knew then that she loved the Beast, and had to return to him.

Putting the magic ring by her bedside, Beauty lay down again and closed her eyes.

When she opened them again, Beauty was back in the Beast's garden - and, true to her dream, he was lying lifeless on the ground.

"Oh, Beast," she cried, taking him in her arms, "please don't die! I love you, and I want to marry you!"

All at once light and music filled the air, and the Beast vanished. In his place stood a handsome prince.

"Who are you?" cried Beauty.

"I was your Beast," said the prince. "An evil witch cast a spell on me and turned me into that poor animal. The spell could only be broken when a beautiful girl agreed to marry me."

A few days later they were married,
and Beauty's family came to join in
the joyous celebrations at the palace.

Beauty had never been so happy. She
loved the prince with all her heart,
and they lived in their rose palace
happily ever after.